I Am Fred

by Nick Rolfe

proudly published by
YOUR STORIES MATTER

First published in 2017 in England by Your Stories Matter

www.rainbowstreetbooks.com

www.yourstoriesmatter.org
hello@yourstoriesmatter.org

Your Stories Matter is an imprint of
Explainer HQ Ltd
Halton Mill
Mill Lane
Lancaster
LA2 6ND
England

This book is printed in the Dyslexie font, the typeface for people with dyslexia, though we find it great for all children. Go to www.dyslexiefont.com to find out more about the typeface.

Fonts used on the cover are courtesy of Khrys Bosland and are available from www.dafont.com

This title is available for sale online and from loads of great bookshops.

A bulk discount is available for educational institutions and charitable organisations through Your Stories Matter.

British Library Cataloguing in Publication Data.
A catalogue record for this book is available from the British Library.

ISBN 978-1-909320-68-0

To both of my beautiful daughters,
Charlie and Tabitha.

***Free* teaching resources**

are available for this book at

www.RainbowStreetBooks.com

There is a street built on love and caring
Kindness, patience, fun and sharing
All homes different, none the same
And Rainbow Street is its name.

The Original Rainbow Street Series:

I Am Fred
The Dandelion Dormice
Mustard and Custard
Basil and Sage
Granny Frogsbottom and the Triplets
Peggy Clover
Lilac and Mauve

Meet Fred. Fred is about your age.

Fred was born a girl. Everyone called him Felicity.

They gave him girl's clothes, girl's toys and girl's things.

Fred looked like a girl.
But inside Fred was a boy.

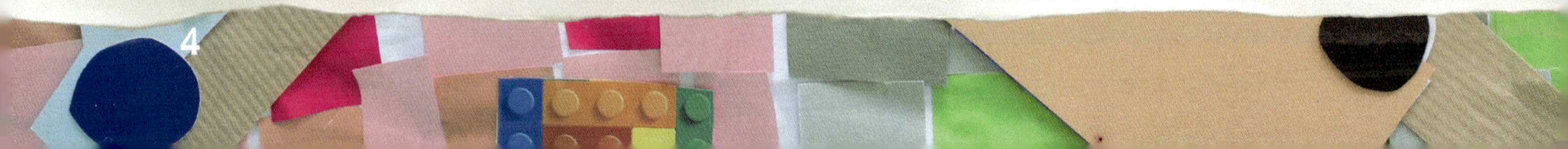

He was a boy trapped inside a girl's body.

Mum always baked Fred a pink birthday cake.

But Fred didn't like pink cake.
Fred didn't like pink at all.

When Mum wasn't looking,
Fred swapped the pink dye for green.

Mum was surprised to see a green cake!
Though Fred ate every crumb.

Mum and Dad bought Fred a pretty doll with long hair.

Fred didn't want a pretty doll.
Fred wanted cars and army things.

So Fred cut the doll's hair off.
Every single bit.

And he dressed her up as a solider.

Mum wanted to buy Felicity a party dress.

There were dresses in every colour.

But Fred didn't want a dress.
He wanted boy's clothes.

No more dresses!
Fred felt better dressed in boy's clothes.

Fred's hair was very long.
Mum liked to brush it and use ribbons.

Fred wanted a haircut.
But Mum and Dad liked it the way it was.

Fred wanted a pet of his very own.
Dad took Fred to a pet shop.

Dad pointed to the fluffy kittens and little bunnies.

Fred didn't want a cute pet.
Fred wanted a scary pet.

Fred chose a spider!
Dad was surprised. And a little scared!

Mum and Dad were worried. Felicity was not like any other girl. They kept getting it wrong.

How could they make her happy?
Fred said: A haircut for a start!

I know you love me and want what's best.

But inside I am a boy.
With a boy's heart and a boy's mind.

I want to live my life as I'm really meant to be.

I am really Fred.
Not Felicity.

Mum and Dad thought very hard.

Mum said: You were meant to be a boy inside and out.

Dad said: We just want you to be happy.

Fred said: Being a boy makes me happy.

Finally, Fred is living as a boy on the inside.
And on the outside.

Now that Fred is happy, everyone is happy.

19:32
yourstoriesmatter.org
YOUR STORIES MATTER
NOV
24
A lovely short film about dyslexia and imagination →
VIDEO
www.YourStoriesMatter.org
sharing experiences | improving understanding | celebrating differences
YSM

20794072R00024

Printed in Great Britain
by Amazon